That New Animal

Emily Jenkins
Pictures by **Pierre Pratt**

FRANCES FOSTER BOOKS

FARRAR, STRAUS AND GIROUX

NEW YORK

FudgeFudge does not like that new animal.
Marshmallow does not like it either. Not even a little bit.
It doesn't seem to be going away.
"Do you smell that new animal smell?" complains FudgeFudge.
"It's very different from a dog smell."

No one has thrown a stick in a long time.
No one has tossed a ball.
The people just sit there, and look at that new animal.
It can't even say "dog" or "sit" or "breakfast" or "bone."

They sit there, and that new animal is using FudgeFudge's spot on the couch.

They sit there, and don't seem to notice that Marshmallow is showing his tummy, all ready to be scratched.

Marshmallow whines,   and is told to pipe down.

FudgeFudge barks,
and is sent to the corner.

But that new animal cries, and is cuddled and kissed.

"Maybe we could eat it," whispers FudgeFudge.

"We'd get in trouble," says Marshmallow.

"Then we'll just bite it."

"No."

"Bite it a LITTLE bit?"

"No."

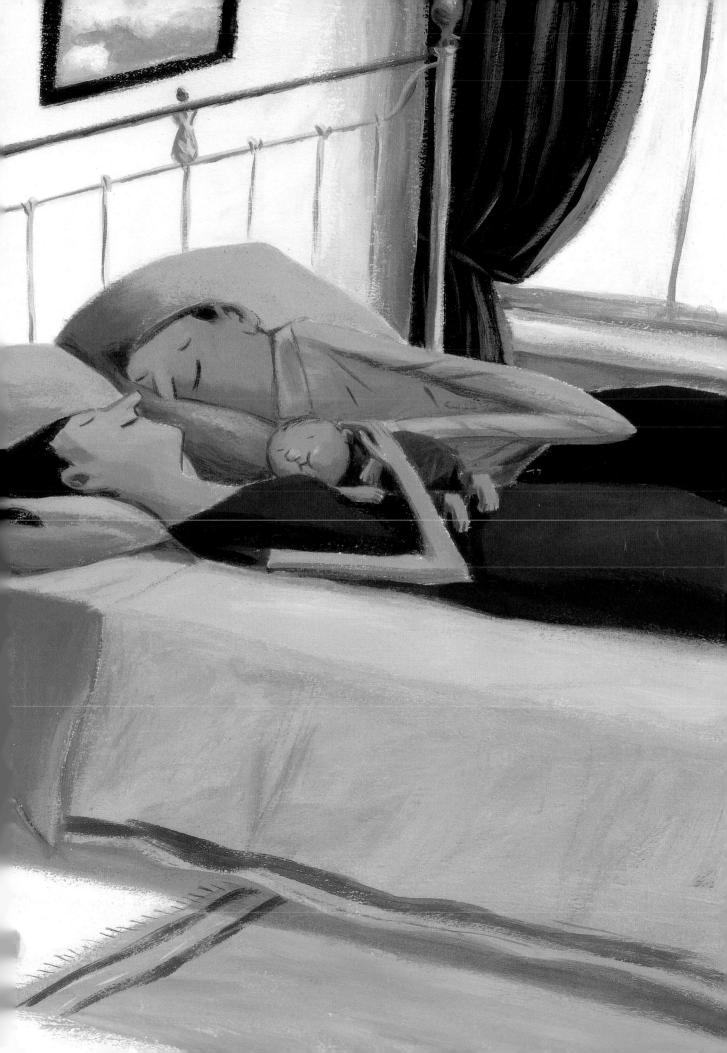

FudgeFudge wants to bury that new animal
under the tree with the dog bones.
Marshmallow tells her no.

FudgeFudge wants to sleep in that new animal's cradle. *On top of the animal.* Marshmallow tells her no.

FudgeFudge chews up three dolls, two board books, and six little outfits before Marshmallow comes in and tells her no.

Marshmallow, tired of saying no all the time
when he hates that new animal as much as anyone,
pees on the carpet in several different places.

"You're a big dog," the people say.
"What's wrong with you?"

Then one morning someone else arrives.
They call him Grandpa. He has a new smell.
Very different from a dog smell.

He is trying to get near that new animal. He wants to pick it up.

FudgeFudge does not think this is a good idea.

Neither does Marshmallow.

They tell him no, barking very loudly.

They will not let this strange Grandpa near that new animal.

No way.

They bark until the Grandpa goes and sits on the other side of the room.

"I thought you hated that animal," whispers FudgeFudge.

"I do," says Marshmallow. "But it's not *his* new animal to go picking up whenever he feels like it. It's *our* animal."

The Grandpa tries again, but Marshmallow scares him off.

"It is our new animal to hate as much as we want to," he tells FudgeFudge.

That afternoon, when the Grandpa is gone, someone throws a stick.
Not for very long, but for a little bit.

And the day after, that new animal looks at FudgeFudge and says "Da," which certainly means "dog."

"It is not such a dumb animal after all," whispers FudgeFudge.

Then one day, Marshmallow finally gets a tummy scratch, and FudgeFudge finds a spot on the couch, a bit farther down from where she used to lie.

It turns out there *is* room for her, as well as for that new animal.

"Marshmallow?" asks FudgeFudge from her place on the couch. "I can't smell that new animal smell. Can you smell that new animal smell?"

No, Marshmallow cannot smell it, either.

It hasn't disappeared, though. That new animal smell has just gotten familiar.

Like dog smell. And people smell. And home smell.

In fact, it is not that *new* animal, anymore, at all.

It is just that animal.

Their animal.

To hate as much as they want to.

And to like, just a little bit.

For Ivy and the cats
— E.J.

Distributed in Canada by Douglas & McIntyre Publishing Group
Color separations by Chroma Graphics PTE Ltd.
Printed and bound in the United States of America by Berryville Graphics
Designed by Jay Colvin
First edition, 2005
10 9 8 7 6 5 4 3

Library of Congress Cataloging-in-Publication Data
Jenkins, Emily, 1967–
    That new animal / Emily Jenkins ; pictures by Pierre Pratt.— 1st ed.
        p.   cm.
    Summary: The lives of two dogs change after a new animal, a baby, comes to
their house.
    ISBN-13: 978-0-374-37443-3
    ISBN-10: 0-374-37443-0
    [1. Dogs—Fiction.   2. Babies—Fiction.]   I. Pratt, Pierre, ill.   II. Title.

PZ7.J4134Th 2005
[E]—dc21
                                                                    2003044058